This book belongs to

Jenny and matthew

Enid Blyton™

My Treasury of FAVOURITE TALES

Published in 2002 by
Alligator Books Limited
155 Regents Park Road
London NW1 8BB

Printed in China

The Newspaper Dog

Once upon a time there was a
little dog called Tips. He belonged to
Mrs. Brown who lived in Primrose
Cottage at the end of Cherry Village.
He was a useful little dog. He
guarded the house each night for
Mrs. Brown. He kept her company
when she was alone. He barked at
any stranger who came up the
front path – and once each
week he fetched a newspaper
for her from old Mr. Jonathan
who lived all by himself in a

little house on the hillside.

Mr. Jonathan always bought the newspaper himself, and read it. Then he lent it to Mrs. Brown, and after that she passed it on to someone else. She couldn't often find time to go to fetch the paper herself, so Tips fetched it for her.

He started off each evening, ran all the way down the village street, went over the bridge that crossed the stream and up the hillside to Mr. Jonathan's cottage. He jumped up at

the door and pushed it open. Then in he would trot and look for Mr. Jonathan.

The old man always had the paper ready for him, neatly folded up with a piece of string round it.

He put the packet into Tips's mouth and off the little dog would go, running all the way home again, not stopping for anything until he reached Primrose Cottage and could drop the paper at Mrs. Brown's feet.

One day Mr. Jonathan thought he would do some spring-cleaning. So he called on Mrs. Brown and asked her to lend him her ladder.

"Dear me, what do you want to go climbing

about on ladders for?" asked Mrs. Brown in surprise. "You'll fall off, Mr. Jonathan, and hurt yourself."

"Indeed I shan't!" said the old man. "I'm going to paint my ceiling white, Mrs. Brown. It is very dirty. So lend me your step-ladder, there's a good soul."

"It's in the shed," said Mrs. Brown. "You can have it if you want it. But do pray be careful, Mr. Jonathan, for it's not a very steady pair of steps."

Mr. Jonathan found the ladder and took it home. He mixed some paint and started to do his ceiling. It looked lovely! All day he worked at it, and then went to bed.

He began again next day, whistling to himself, sloshing about on the ceiling with the paint quite enjoying himself. And then a dreadful thing happened.

The postman dropped some letters in the letterbox and gave such a loud rat-a-tat that the shock made old Mr. Jonathan fall off his ladder. Down he went – and when he tried to get up he found that he couldn't.

"Oh dear, oh dear, I must have sprained my ankle, or

broken my leg, or something," the old man groaned.

"Whatever shall I do? Nobody else will come today, and I can't phone for the doctor. I have no neighbours to call to. I am all alone!"

Mr. Jonathan lay there on the floor, groaning. He really didn't know what he was going to do.

Perhaps he would have to stay there all night long. If only somebody would come! But there was nobody to come at all. And then, just as he was thinking that, Mr. Jonathan heard the sound of pitter-pattering feet, and someone came running up the front path. Then a little body hurled itself against the door which opened at once. It was Tips, the little newspaper dog, coming to get the evening paper!

He saw Mr. Jonathan lying on the floor, and, he was puzzled. He ran up to him and licked his hand. Then he

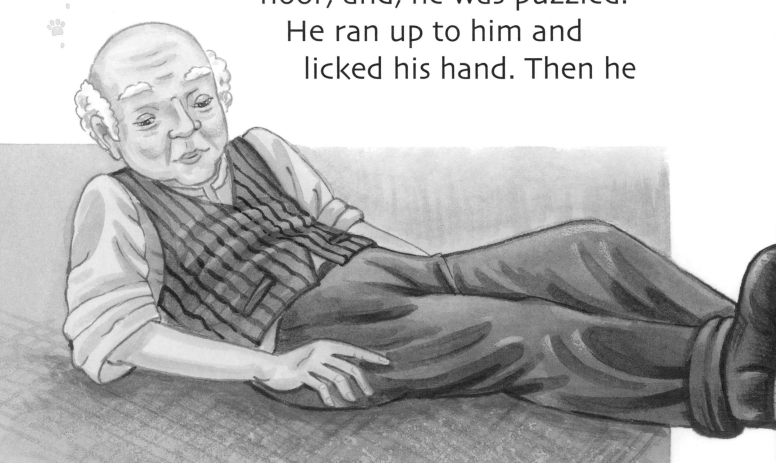

sat down with his head on one side and said, "Woof!"

That was his way of saying: "What's the matter? Can I help you?"

"I wish you could, Tips," said Mr. Jonathan. And then he suddenly looked more cheerful. Perhaps Tips *could* help him. He looked round. The newspaper was on a chair, already tied up with string for Mrs. Jones.

"There's the paper, Tips," said Mr. Jonathan, pointing. "Fetch it here!"

Tips saw the paper, and took it into his mouth. He was just going to run off with it when Mr. Jonathan called him back.

"Don't go yet, Tips," he said.

"Bring the paper here."

The clever little dog understood. He ran over to Mr. Jonathan with the paper in his mouth. Mr. Jonathan took a pencil from his pocket and wrote in large letters across the top of the paper:

"Mrs. Brown. I have fallen off the ladder. Please fetch the doctor. Mr. Jonathan."

Then he pushed the paper once more into Tips's mouth and patted the waiting dog. "Go home now," he said.

Tips ran off, puzzling his little head to know why Mr. Jonathan was on the floor. He ran to Mrs. Brown as soon as he reached Primrose Cottage and dropped the paper at her feet. She picked it up, and caught sight of the message scribbled on the top.

"Good gracious me," she cried. "Poor old Mr. Jonathan! He's tumbled off the ladder!"

She sent for the doctor at once, and he took her along to Mr. Jonathan's in his car. It wasn't long before they had him safely in bed, his leg bandaged up, and a nice hot drink beside him.

"It was my clever little dog Tips who found Mr. Jonathan when he came for my paper this evening," said Mrs. Brown proudly to the doctor.

"Mr. Jonathan wrote a message on the paper, and, of course, I saw it when Tips dropped the paper at my feet."

Mr. Jonathan soon got well, and one morning Mrs. Brown and Tips met him going shopping for the first time, leaning on a stick.

"Now wherever are you going?" cried Mrs. Brown. "I'm sure there's no shopping so important that I can't do it for you. Whatever is it you must buy, Mr. Jonathan?"

"It's something very special," said

Mr. Jonathan with a smile, and he
went into a little shop nearby
beckoning Tips and Mrs. Brown in

too. And what do you suppose the special bit of shopping was? Why, a fine red collar for Tips!

"That's to show everyone what a clever, helpful little chap he is," said Mr. Jonathan, putting it round the little dog's neck. "He really does deserve it."

I think so, too, don't you?

The Tale of Flop and Whiskers

Flop and Whiskers were two white rabbits belonging to Ben and Jane. They had fine whiskers, little black bobtails and big floppy ears. Ben and Jane were very fond of them and looked after them well.

Flop and Whiskers lived happily enough in a big hutch. They were friendly with one another, but sometimes they found things dull.

"Oh, if only something exciting would happen!" Flop would sigh.

"Yes, something that we could remember and talk about for weeks and weeks," said Whiskers. "But nothing ever happens to pet rabbits. They live in a hutch and eat and sleep. That's all."

But one night something *did* happen! Flop and Whiskers heard a noise in the garden, and looked out of their hutch. There was bright moonlight and coming down the garden path was a long procession of fairies. In their midst was a snow-white carriage with gold handles and gold wheels. It was drawn by six rabbits.

"Just look at that!" cried Flop, excitedly. "It must be a fairy

princess of some kind. Oh, don't I wish I was one of those rabbits pulling her carriage! Wouldn't I feel grand!"

"Isn't it beautiful?" said Whiskers, his little nose pressed against the wires of the hutch door.

The procession came down the path and passed by the rabbits' cage. They were so excited. They could see a princess in the snow-white carriage

and just as she passed their hutch she leaned out and blew a kiss to them. Flop scraped at the wire of the door, trying her hardest to get out and run after the procession – but it was no use, the wire was too strong.

"Look!" suddenly cried Whiskers. "The procession has stopped. What has happened?"

"One of the rabbits has gone lame," said Flop. "See, its foot is limping."

What a to-do there was! All the fairies gathered around the limping rabbit, who shook his head dolefully and held up his foot in pain.

The princess leaned out of her carriage and pointed to the rabbit hutch she had just passed. She called out something in her high little voice.

"I say, Flop, I believe the princess is saying that one of us could draw her carriage instead of the lame rabbit!" said Whiskers, in excitement. "Oh, I wonder which of us will be chosen."

The little fairies came running back to the rabbit hutch and climbed up to the wire.

"Will you come and draw our princess's carriage just for tonight?" they cried. "One of our rabbits has hurt its foot."

"Oh yes!" squeaked the two white rabbits in delight. "But which of us do you want?"

"Both of you, please," said the fairies. "You see the rabbits have to go on in pairs, and we can't leave the lame rabbit alone. We shall set free the hurt rabbit and his companion, so that we can have you two white rabbits instead. So will you both come? You shall be brought back before sunrise."

Flop and Whiskers joyfully told the fairies how to open their hutch and then they jumped out in delight. In a moment they were

harnessed with the other rabbits, and
the two whose place they were
taking, hopped away into the hedges.
The fairies cried out in delight to see
the two beautiful white rabbits
among the other ones.

They made such a noise that they
woke up Ben and Jane. The children

jumped out of bed and went to their bedroom window, looking out into the moonlight.

They saw the fairy procession going along down the garden path and they stared in astonishment.

"Jane!" said Ben, "look at those white rabbits, drawing the carriage along with the four other rabbits. Don't they look like Flop and Whiskers."

"Yes, they do," said Jane. "And oh,

look! Ben, their hutch door is open. I can see it quite plainly in the moonlight."

The children ran downstairs to see the procession, but it had passed by before they were in the garden. So they went to see if the rabbit hutch was open – and it was.

"Oh dear, I *shall* be sorry not to have dear old Flop and Whiskers," said Jane, almost crying. "They were so sweet. I don't think it was very kind of the fairies to take them away from us."

But the next morning the hutch door was fast shut and the two white rabbits were safely back in their hutch once more!

When Ben and Jane went to peep, they found both rabbits fast asleep in the hay, and they didn't even wake up when the children put some fresh lettuce in for them.

"Goodness, aren't they tired!" said Jane. "I expect they walked for miles last night, dragging that lovely carriage behind them. I do wonder where they went."

Where *did* they go?
Well, they went to a
party! The Prince of
Derry-Down Palace
was just twenty-one
and he had sent out
invitations to his birthday party –
and, of course, the Princess had one of
the beautiful invitation cards too.

Her name was Fenella, and she
loved parties. She had only just grown
up, so she hadn't been to many big

parties. She had a new dress and new silver shoes made, and she looked very lovely in them.

"I will lend you my second-best coach, the white one with gold wheels," said her father, the King. "And you shall have either my six rabbits to draw it, or my six cats." The Princess chose the rabbits, and they were the very ones that the two children had seen in the night. The two white rabbits, Flop and Whiskers, watched the two whose place they took, run into the hedge, and then off they went with the other four.

"I hope we keep up all right," panted Flop. "We aren't very used to galloping, we've been so used to sitting in our hutch."

But they galloped along just as fast as the other rabbits, and the Princess was very pleased. "They shall go to the Rabbits' Party," she said to the fairies with her. "They deserve it."

The Prince was giving a party

for his friends and the rabbits he
sometimes rode were giving a party
for the six rabbits who drew the
Princess's coach – so you can imagine
the delight of Flop and Whiskers
when four fine rabbits with bows
round their necks, made them
welcome to their own little party in
the grounds of the palace!

The rabbits were given blue bows

to wear, and sat down at little tables with dishes of delicious looking food.

"Look, Flop," said Whiskers. "Carrot Sandwiches!"

"And see – that's Cabbage Pie!" said Flop. "And here's Turnip Cake. And what's this – Lettuce Biscuits! What a wonderful meal!"

It certainly was – and afterwards the ten rabbits had a little dance of their own. Flop and Whiskers were very sorry when it was all over. The rabbits pulled the Princess's carriage home for her – and then they ran back to their hutch and curled up to go to sleep, tired out!

Flop and Whiskers longed to tell the children all about their adventures, but they couldn't. When they woke up they looked at one another in delight, and Flop said, "Did we dream it, Whiskers, or

was it true?"

"Quite true," said Whiskers. "We had an adventure at last, Flop. We can talk about it for weeks and weeks, and we'll never feel dull again."

So Flop and Whiskers talk about it all day long – and I wish I could listen to them, don't you?

The Mouse and the Squirrel

There was a little mouse who lived in a hole in a ditch. He ran about all night long, looking for titbits everywhere – and one night he went into a cottage and sniffed about for a bit of bacon or piece of cheese.

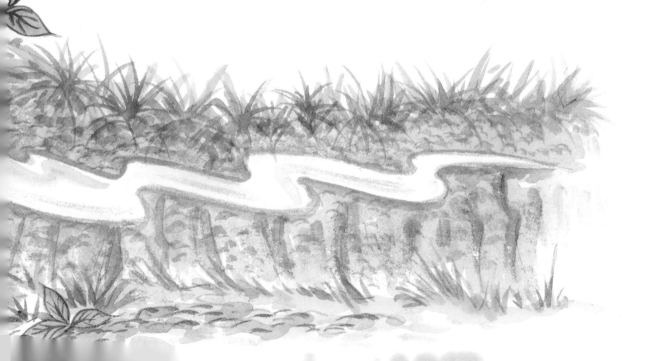

Aha! What was this? Bacon rind, smelling fresh and delicious! The mouse ran to it and began to nibble. But alas! It was a trap; and there came a loud rap as the trap worked, and tried to catch the little mouse. He leapt backwards, but his front foot was caught and badly hurt.

The little mouse squealed and pulled his foot away. Then, limping badly, he hurried out of the cottage by the hole through which he had come, and went back to the wood. His foot made him feel very ill, for it pained him.

He could not go out hunting for grain and seeds as he used to do. He was hungry and wondered if he could ask for help from someone.

By his hole he saw a fat grey squirrel who was sitting up on his hind legs, his bushy tail well in the air, nibbling at an acorn.

"Good-day, squirrel," said the

mouse humbly. "Could you spare me an acorn? Or could you get me a scarlet hip from the wild-rose bramble over there? I have hurt my foot and cannot go hunting for food. I am very hungry."

"What!" cried the squirrel, in a rage. "You, a mouse, dare to ask a grey squirrel for a favour like that! Of course I shall not get food for you!

Do you think I am a servant of mice?
The idea of asking such a thing!"

"I do not mean to be uncivil," said
the mouse. "It is only that I have hurt
my foot and cannot get food."

"Then ask someone else to do your
hunting for you!" said the selfish
squirrel, and bounded off.

The little mouse sat at the entrance
to his burrow and watched the

squirrel. It was autumn and the little grey creature was storing away tiny heaps of nuts here and there, so that when he awoke for a few warm days now and then in the winter-time he could go to his hidden stores, have a feast, and then go to sleep again.

He hid some acorns behind the ivy-bark. He put some nuts under a pile of leaves in the ditch. He scraped a little hole under the roots of the oak tree and put four nuts there. He went to the hollow tree nearby and hid seven acorns. He was well prepared for warm days in the winter!

The mouse wished he could go and take some of the nuts – but he could

not move far without pain. He lay in his hole and nearly starved. Then another mouse ran by, and saw the thin and hungry one.

"What's the matter," he asked, running into the hole.

The little mouse soon told him. The other mouse listened.

"Well, you know," he said, "I would dearly love to help you, but I have a

large and hungry family, and it is all I can do to find food for them. It is very scarce this year."

"I know where plenty of food is!" said the little mouse eagerly. "Get it for me, and we will all share it! Look for acorns behind the ivy-bark, and in the hollow tree. Hunt under the leaves in the ditch for nuts, and under the roots of the oak tree opposite! I saw the squirrel put some there!"

The other mouse ran off in glee. Sure enough he found nuts and acorns in plenty. He carried them one by one to his own hole, fetched the first mouse, and helped him along to the hole too. Then, with all the mouse family, the first little mouse ate in peace. Soon his leg was quite well, and he could run about happily once more.

The grey squirrel slept
soundly until the month of
January, when there was a
warm spell. He awoke and went
to find his nuts – but alas for
him! However hard he looked, he
could *not* find anything to eat at
all! His cupboards were empty, each
one! He went back to his tree,
hungry, and slept again.

Then February came, and the sun
sent warm fingers into the tree where
the squirrel slept soundly. Once again
he awoke and came scampering down,

hungry as a hunter!

He searched behind the ivy-bark – no acorns there! He hunted in the ditch – no nuts there! He looked in the hollow tree – no acorns to be seen! And last of all he put his little paw in the hole he had made beneath the roots of the oak tree. No – not a nut to be

found. He must go hungry.

"I shall starve!" he said, in fright. And then he suddenly caught sight of the little mouse, who was now plump and sleek. The squirrel called to him:

"Oh, mouse, you are fat! Let me have a little of your food, I beg you! I am lean and hungry, and I cannot find any of the food I stored away. I must have looked in the wrong places!"

"Last autumn I asked *you* for a little food!" said the mouse, stopping. "But you said no! Why should I help you now?"

"You are right," said the squirrel sadly. "I treated you badly. There is no reason why you should not treat me the same."

"Wait!" said the mouse. "There *is* a reason why I should not treat you the same, squirrel! You and I are not alike! You are selfish and greedy, but I am not. You shall share what I have!"

He brought the squirrel two nuts and an acorn. The squirrel thanked the mouse humbly, and vowed that he would repay the mouse when he found his own stores that he had hidden away.

"I was lucky this winter," said the little mouse, with a gleam in his eye. "I found four heaps of nuts and acorns – one behind the ivy-bark – one in the ditch – one in the hollow tree – and one under the roots of the oak. So I and my friends have feasted well!"

The squirrel listened. At first he was

angry, but then he remembered that, after all, the mouse had let him have some food.

"So these are *my* nuts and *my* acorn!" he said. "Well – I deserved to lose them for my greed! Forgive me, mouse! Next autumn I will store up a hoard for you too!"

He kept his word, and now he and the mouse are great friends, and if you see one, you will know that the other is somewhere nearby.

The Tale of Cluck and Clopper

"There's that dog again!" said Cluck the hen, and she ran away at top speed. All the other hens scuttled away too. Tinker the dog was a tease. He loved chasing the hens and seeing them scamper off in fright.

He chased them now, first into one corner of the farmyard and then into another. What a time he had, barking and prancing!

One little hen squeezed through a gap in the hedge, and went into the field where the horses were kept. She found herself near a big horse who looked at the clucking hen in surprise.

"What's the matter?" said the horse.

"It's that dog," said the hen. "Can't you hear him chasing all the hens? We get so frightened. You see, if he caught one of us he might bite us!"

"Well, stay by me," said the horse. "What's your name? Mine is Clopper."

"Mine is Cluck," said the hen. "I think I'm alright here. I'll just take a walk round this field and see if I

can scratch up something to eat."

So she set off by herself, looking into all the corners – and then, quite suddenly, she saw Tinker the dog squeezing through the hedge near her. He had seen her through the leaves. Aha! Another hen to chase!

Cluck scampered away clucking loudly. Tinker pinned her into a corner, with a bush behind her. "Cluck, cluck – cluck, cackle, cackle, CLUCK!" she cried. "Help, help!"

Clopper the horse looked up and saw what was happening. He cantered over at once and neighed. Then he said "HROOOOOOMPH" just like that, and Tinker stopped prancing about and looked astonished.

"Off with you!" said Clopper, stamping his hoof. "I said OFF WITH YOU! HROOOOOOMPH!"

Tinker fled for his life,

yelping. What an enormous animal a horse was when it stood right over you! Tinker didn't like it at all.

"Thank you, Clopper. Thank you very much," said Cluck, gratefully. "One of these days perhaps, I can do

you a good turn – and help you."

Clopper gave a loud neighing laugh. "What! A little thing like you help a great big thing like me! Nonsense! You're not so important as all that, little hen – you could never be of any use to me."

"Well – one good turn deserves

another," said Cluck, "I would dearly *like* to help you, Clopper."

She went off back to the farm – but often after that she came into the horse's field to see her big friend, and pecked happily between his feet.

Clopper didn't mind. The little hen amused him. She asked him all kinds of questions.

"Why do you have such big feet with no claws or toes? Why do you wear a mane of hair? And dear me, Clopper, why is your tail cut so short? All the other horses have long tails that swish to and fro."

"Mine's docked," said Clopper. "That means that it's been cut very short to make me look smart. I'm the only horse with a docked tail.

Don't you think I look smart?"

"Yes," said Cluck, who thought Clopper was the smartest, cleverest, kindest horse in the world. "It does seem silly to wear a long tail when you can have it cut short and look so neat."

But, when the hot summer days came, Cluck changed her mind about tails. There were flies everywhere that month. Oh what a nuisance they were to the horses and the cows! They flew down to them in clouds, and walked about all over the big creatures, and often bit them. The cows swung their long tails to and fro and beat them off.

The horses swished their hairy tails, flicking off dozens of flies at a time. How glad they were to have long tails then! But Clopper couldn't swish away the flies, because his tail was short. He had to stand in the field and feel them running all over him and often biting him. He couldn't bear it! He scampered here and he scampered there, trying to shake the flies off his back. He reared and he stamped – but as soon as he had scared the flies away, down they came

again! Cluck was very sorry for him.
How she wished he had a proper tail.
Poor Clopper!

One morning she went to him, "Clopper, I've thought of a way to help you. You said you'd never need my help, but you do. Listen, will you please lie down in the grass and let me show you what I can do?"

Clopper lay down in surprise. The flies flew down to him as soon as he was still. Then little Cluck hopped up on to his back. "Keep still, Clopper, keep still!" she clucked. "I'm going to peck up and eat every fly I see! Keep still!"

Clopper felt Cluck's little feet running up and down his back and she pecked up flies here, there and everywhere! Oh how wonderful! Not one was biting him now, not one was annoying him!

"I've eaten every one," said Cluck. "And I believe they're scared of me now. They're not flying down, anyway. I'll just sit myself in the middle of your back, Clopper, and wait till more come – then I'll be after them again."

And do you know, every single day after that Cluck went to jump on Clopper's back to help him with all the flies.

Don't you think it was a very, very good idea? "You see, I was right!" said Cluck. "Little things can help big things!"

Yes, you are right, Cluck. You certainly are a good friend to Clopper. I wondered what you were doing up there on his back! Now I know!